Davina Dupree Suspects a Smuggler

Fourth in the Egmont school series

S K Sheridan

Monday, 6th February

Greetings, Diary!

Arabella and I have just come back from a meeting with our EXTREMELY strict science teacher, Mrs Bunsen. It was held in her science laboratory – or lab as we call it here - which is in the north wing of our term-time home, Egmont Exclusive Boarding School for Girls. All us first years were there, our tummies rumbling away loudly because we could smell the rosemary and garlic potatoes and roast lamb that Marcel is cooking for our dinner. #Mmmmmm #SUCH a yummy smell.

The lab is ENORMOUS and has a glass ceiling - we have astronomy classes there once a week where we study the stars. They're quite fun lessons because we're allowed to lie on our backs on the desks as long as we're concentrating on the stars in our galaxy, the Milky Way, (SUCH a funny name.com) but Mrs Bunsen is tremendously strict about manners and if any one falls asleep and starts snoring she clears her throat very loudly in their ear and they have to leave and go to bed! #Scaryteacher, #Learningfail.

In the middle of the room there are long wooden desks with white basins fitted into them where we wash all the science equipment when we've finished doing experiments. Mrs Bunsen usually marches up and down the classroom at this point, handing out tea-towels and checking that each piece of equipment is bone dry. She's very small, always wears her silver hair in a tight bun and NEVER smiles! Her thin lips are set into a thin line and remain like this even when the whole class has done really well in a test or something. I find her a bit terrifying to be honest, but my best friend Arabella really likes her and in return Mrs Bunsen has a soft spot for Arabella. I know this because I saw Mrs Bunsen *almost* smile once when Arabella was working out a ridiculously complicated chemistry equation on the board. I think they understand each other, what with their mutual love of science and maths. Personally, I'm more at home in the art room with Miss Wise and Miss Cherry. #More relaxing, #Less shouty.

Anyway, Mrs Bunsen had called today's meeting to discuss an important science experiment that we'll soon be doing on the beach at Little Pineham.

'Sit down, be quiet,' she barked as we all filed into the lab. "Hand me that hairbrush Cleo, you can have it back at the end of the meeting. Stop looking at your nails, Clarice, I want to see *every single person* in this room looking at me so I know that they're listening properly.'

Arabella and I chose velvet and gold padded stools next to the twins, Moira and Lynne. When everyone was assembled and we were being so quiet you could have heard a pin drop on the white, shiny floor, Mrs Bunsen tapped a key on her laptop and a giant photograph of Little Pineham beach flashed on to the wall.

'This,' Mrs Bunsen said, hitting the wall with a long, pointy stick. 'Is where we will be going tomorrow to set up our experiment. And this,' she tapped another key on her laptop and an image of our school's kitchen's flashed up, complete with Head Chef Marcel pulling a funny face. 'Is where our journey will begin.'

'That's really silly Mrs Bunsen,' Clarice said, still looking at her nails. Cleo and Clarice are the most ANNOYING girls in the school. They think they're SO amazing and beautiful, but they're not very nice to anyone, especially me and Arabella. 'The beach isn't in the kitchen is it?'

'Sapphires loses one house point because Clarice called out without putting up her hand,' Mrs Bunsen said.

'Shut *up*, will you?' Arabella hissed loudly in Clarice's direction. I noticed Mrs Bunsen flicking a glance at Arabella but luckily she didn't say anything. Cleo and Clarice are ALWAYS losing us house points which Arabella really minds about because she's very competitive and wants Sapphires to win the House Shield this term. Emeralds won it last term, and I don't think poor Rubies have EVER won it. #Not very sporty.

Melody put her hand up.

'Yes?' Mrs Bunsen pointed the stick at her.

'Um, on the letter you sent my parents about the school trip you mentioned that there are old smuggling tunnels that lead from the school's kitchen cellars down to the beach at Little Pineham,' Melody said, going red.

'Excellent, one house point to Sapphires,' Mrs Bunsen nodded grimly. Arabella gave Melody the thumbs up. 'Well remembered Melody, you are absolutely correct. Bertie the gardener told me about the tunnels a few months ago when he discovered that someone, probably Marcel, had moved a stack of crates hiding an old door in the deepest, darkest kitchen cellar. He opened the door and came face to face with a black tunnel, which he bravely decided to go down, armed with a powerful torch. He followed the tunnel all the way to its end and came out on

Little Pineham beach. On the way back, he shone his torch at the walls and saw old graffiti there that smugglers had written hundreds of years ago. I myself have investigated the tunnel and can confirm that there are indeed messages scratched into the wall, saying things like, "Old Seamus left ten quarts of brandy from The Crimson Wave ship int' big house's veg garden for Young Jimny, 22nd December, 1756".'

'Oh I see,' I called out, feeling excited. Then I remembered about Mrs Bunsen's strict no calling out rule and put my hand up.

'Do share, Davina,' she said, eyebrows lowering.

'I think the message means that a smuggler called Old Seamus took or stole some bottles of brandy from a ship called The Crimson Wave, smuggled them through the secret tunnel and left them hidden in the grounds of the big house, which is probably now our school, for someone called Young Jimny, nearly three hundred years ago.' I said, ignoring the faces Cleo and Clarice were making at me.

'Precisely,' Mrs Bunsen agreed dryly. 'You should be a detective, Davina.' I nodded in agreement, because I *am* nearly a detective as Arabella and I have already solved several mysteries together in the past.

Cleo put her hand up.

'I hope you don't expect *us* to travel down this revolting tunnel, Mrs Bunsen?' she said.

'That's precisely what I expect you to do, Cleo,' Mrs Bunsen looked almost cheerful as Cleo and Clarice shot each other horrified glances. 'We will all assemble outside the school's kitchen door tomorrow morning at nine o'clock sharp. Late comers will lose points for their houses. Each of you must be wearing a rainproof coat and wellies, with sensible clothes underneath. I will provide you with head torches so you can pick your way through the tunnel without any fuss. Mrs Bunn, Egmont's new dinner lady, has kindly agreed to come with us to provide an extra pair of hands, so I trust you will all make her feel welcome. I'll tell you what the experiment actually involves when we get to the beach, and needless to say I'll be bringing essential items like anti-explosive aprons and safety goggles.'

Arabella grinned madly at this news and I felt quite excited about seeing the old smuggling messages. Cleo and Clarice had gone pale yellow and looked like they were going to either throw up or faint. Dark tunnels weren't really their idea of fun. #No mirrors.

'That's all for now, first years,' Mrs Bunsen shut her laptop smartly and surveyed us with her eagle eyes. 'You are dismissed. You may file out quietly.'

Tuesday, 7th February

Good morning Diary!

Well! Last night Arabella and I were finishing off our particularly delish roast dinners while we tried to guess what the science experiment might be, when all of a sudden a bit of drama blew up.

'You idiot,' Clarice screeched, jumping up and flapping her arms about. Arabella and I stood up to get a better view of what was going on. The new trainee chef, Franco, was standing next to Clarice, beetroot red. Clarice's white top had been drenched in a green goo, which was dripping off her into thick puddles on the floor. I felt quite sorry for Franco, he looks quite small and youngish and he was shaking with nerves.

'Good shot, Franco,' Arabella whispered, grinning. 'He must have tripped and accidentally thrown mint sauce all over her!'

'What eez all this fuss about, please?' Came Marcel's loud voice from the kitchen. The metal doors banged open and the head chef came cantering out. He threw his hands in the air when he saw Clarice's top.

'Franco! Why you do this to me?' Marcel shouted. 'I give you job as a favour to your father, and this is 'ow you repay me? We put the food on the *table*, Franco, not on the pupils' clothes. Now go and get a cloth this *instant*.'

Franco dithered around for a moment, then stumbled off towards the kitchen. #Poor chap.

'I don't want a *cloth*!' Clarice screamed. 'My

top is ruined. RUINED. Mummy bought it back from St Tropez and it cost her five hundred euros and I'll never be able to get another one like it, it was an original! I'm going off to change.' And with that she flounced out, closely followed by Cleo who was also flouncing, just for effect.

Mrs Fairchild, the headmistress, who'd been tucking into her food quite happily while the drama unfolded, stood up, gave a little burp and clapped her hands. 'Sit down everybody please, the pantomime's over,' she trilled. #Eccentric lady.

'Mmm, look Davina,' Arabella pointed to the end of our table where a chef was carefully putting down two silver bowls. 'Our Magic Mousse has arrived. I could seriously eat it for breakfast, lunch and dinner for the rest of my life, it's so unbelievably yummy.' Magic Mousse is Arabella's favourite EVER dessert. It's made from special, glittery sweets that

Marcel says he orders from Italy, which are crushed up and stirred into a dark chocolate sauce. The sauce is then poured over a honeycomb sponge cake, so that it soaks in and oozes out of the bottom. I think it's very tasty but Arabella likes it more; she goes into a kind of trance when she's eating it and doesn't talk till her bowl is scraped clean. #VERY interesting to watch!

Mrs Bunn, the new dinner lady, patrolled the dining hall while we ate, chewing a strawberry smelling sweet. I kept getting whiffs of it whenever she walked past. She's small and squashy looking, with wispy white hair pinned back in a bun. Mrs Bunn wears a bun! It's a bit like Mrs Bunsen's only not as neat. She kept on and on smiling at everyone, but I couldn't help noticing that when Franco was being told off by Marcel, her eyes stopped being smiley and turned narrow, and she edged closer to hear what was going on. Oh well, maybe she's short sighted.

Ooh, I can't wait to go down the tunnel, I'm already dressed in my coat and wellies. Actually I'm beginning to get a bit hot... #Perhaps I should have waited...

Lunch time, Tuesday 7th February

Wow, what a day, Diary!

Arabella and I made it to the science lab this morning with only minutes to spare because it took ages to find Arabella's wellies (eventually located behind the mess under her bed, #typical), earning us a poisonous look from Mrs Bunsen. She was in the middle of handing out head torches, so we took one each and strapped them onto our foreheads, then we couldn't stop laughing because we looked so silly! Mrs Bunsen didn't think it was funny though, I don't think she's got much of a sense of humour. Cleo and Clarice refused to wear theirs, so Mrs Bunn, who was already wearing a head torch, together with pink and white wellies and a green quilted raincoat, said;

'Come on, duckies, you don't want to trip and hurt yourselves in the tunnel do you?'

'How hard can it be to walk in a straight line?' Cleo replied, rude as always, and Mrs Bunn scowled, making her face look really different from usual, sort of glaring and cross instead of plump and crinkly.

We marched off to the kitchens in single file, led by Mrs Bunsen who was in sergeant major mode, and found Marcel was waiting for us with our packed lunches.

'Smoked salmon and avocado sandwiches, Belgian chocolate truffles, exotic fruit medley, beetroot crisps and fizzy grape juice in each one,' he smiled proudly, stroking his moustache. 'Ok girls, follow me and please don't touch anything in the cellars, I keep my Italian sweets for Magic Mousse down there and they're so expensive we can't afford to 'ave even one jar smashed, yes?'

'Yes Marcel,' Arabella nodded her head seriously.

Going down into the cellars was like going into Aladdin's Cave. We stepped carefully down a winding, gold staircase, 'oohing' and 'aahing' at all the piles of unusual food stacked everywhere. Old fashioned lamps attached to the cellar walls provided a dim glimmer which made all the bottles and jars look like mysterious treasure.

'Look, those are jars of rare herbs that Marcel puts on chicken,' Melony said, pointing to about fifty large jars full of red, amber and dark green leaves.

'And those must be his seaweed pasta shells,' Moira said, as we passed a stack of large packets containing gold and green shapes.

We walked on, going deeper and deeper underground.

'Yippee, sweets for Magic Mousse,' Arabella said, licking her lips as we entered the last cellar. She stopped and stared at a stack of about two hundred silver lidded jars absolutely packed with glittery sweets in extraordinary, twisty shapes. 'Listen everyone, walk past these jars really carefully, OK?' She stood with her arms stretched out protectively while we walked past.

'Stop here, first years,' Mrs Bunsen boomed loudly. 'Arms by your sides, eyes on me. *Absolutely* no talking.' I tore my eyes away from the sweets and saw that she'd positioned herself, soldier like, in front of a battered looking wooden door. 'This is the door to the old smuggling tunnel,' Mrs Bunsen glared round at us, almost as though she thought WE were the smugglers who'd dug the tunnel. 'So best behaviour from now on and NO pushing once we've set off, the tunnel is *very* narrow in places and I don't want any accidents. Thank you for your help Marcel.' She nodded at the chef.

Marcel, who was standing near to me and Arabella, bowed theatrically and took down a large key from a shelf. He unlocked the door and pushed it open, revealing the big, dark mouth of the tunnel. A whoosh of cold, salty air blew onto our faces and we all shivered. #Seaweedy.

'Mmm,' Melody said, taking in deep breaths. 'I can smell the sea already.'

'Single file and off we go!' Mrs Bunsen roared, switching on her head torch and stepping into the tunnel. Arabella and I switched on ours and walked into the darkness behind her, followed by Melody, Lynne, Moira and Lottie then the rest of the first years.

I could hear Mrs Bunn talking in a kind way to Cleo and Clarice right at the back. 'Come on you two, it's only a harmless tunnel, for goodness sake. Honestly, I've never met two bigger wimps in all my life.'

'Do you *realise* I'm missing my helicopter flying lesson in order to stagger down this stinking tunnel?' Clarice whined in reply. I heard lurching and slipping noises. 'This is SO not my idea of fun.'

Our head torches were quite strong and gave off enough light for us to study the eerie green and black, slimy walls. Choppy axe marks were everywhere and there was even one whole axe sticking out of a particularly rough looking wall. Mrs Bunsen had been right about the old fashioned graffiti – the walls were littered with scratchy writing that said things like, "One eyed Amos smuggled here, 1799", "Five tons of whiskey waitin' for Billy at the house, 16th October 1753", and "Mack Mousel lost 'is axe here on 3rd April 1802". The more I read and the further down the tunnel we went, the faster and louder my heart beat, until I thought EVERYONE must be able to hear it. It was like going back in time, seeing actual smuggling messages. I was just beginning to feel a little scared when...

'Agh,' Cleo screamed. There was a thump.

'Oh get up,' came Mrs Bunn's voice. She sounded like she was chewing – probably one of those strawberry sweets again. 'For goodness sake, ducks, grow up and turn your head torch on. Then you'll be able to see and you'll stop sliding all over the place.'

'Never!' Cleo shouted. 'It's a crime to fashion.'

'Please yourself,' Mrs Bunn clucked in reply. 'But don't blame me if your raincoat gets covered in slimy moss from the tunnel floor, you silly ninny. And why you're wearing high heeled wellies is beyond me.'

'Hrmph!' Cleo snorted.

I lost track of time and for a little while it seemed like we'd be trooping through the tunnel forever, sometimes upwards, sometimes downwards, sometimes through narrow bits, sometimes through wide caves. Mrs Bunsen stopped in one particularly large cave to show us the pointy rocks that hung down like sharks teeth from the cave's roof.

'These are called stalactites,' she boomed, her voice echoing off the walls. 'Remember that name, I'll be testing you on it next week.'

'Slave driver,' Cleo hissed.

Eventually a pin prick of light appeared in front of us and within minutes we'd reached the end of the tunnel and stepped out into a cold, blustery February day. A mixture of grey and white puffy clouds billowed across the silvery sky, while curved waves raced each other over a slate coloured sea. The long stretch of sand that made up Little Pineham's beach looked damp and blotchy as though it had recently been rained on. A few drops fell onto my face as if to prove this fact and I pulled my warm coat round me even tighter, hoisting the hood over my head. High cliffs loomed to the right of the sand and as I walked on I saw that our tunnel entrance was carved into one of these. There were other caves set into the cliff's base too, some quite deep looking and I shivered with excitement, loving the mysterious sight of them.

'Gather round, first years,' Mrs Bunsen strode into the middle of the sand and zipped up her waterproof coat, tying the hood tightly under her chin, her bun causing a mound of blue canvas to loom up at the back, alien-style. She put her hands on her hips and stared at us until we were all assembled in front of her, Mrs Bunn ushering the angry looking Cleo and Clarice ahead of her. They were having trouble tottering over the sand in their high heeled wellies, most hilarious.com. 'Now,' Mrs Bunsen went on. 'I shall explain the science experiment to you so please listen *very* carefully because if it's not done correctly it could be *extremely* dangerous. I don't want to have to call any ambulances.' We all nodded. #Scary teacher.

'Right,' she said. 'I hope you all remember what we learnt last week about the sun?'

'Ooh, me, me, me!' Arabella's hand shot up and she jumped up and down.

'Yes Arabella?' Mrs Bunsen said.

'The sun creates solar energy,' Arabella said. 'The light from it takes eight minutes to reach the earth and we turn it into electricity. I read a book about it after your lesson.'

'Swot,' Clarice whispered. She's just jealous, the mean thing. She always says things like that to anyone who gets better grades than her.

'Well done, Arabella,' Mrs Bunsen said, the corners of her mouth tweaking upwards ever so slightly. 'Today we're going to create our own energy, right here on this beach. A little bit like the sun does, only in reverse. Mrs Bunn, do you have the anti-explosive aprons?'

'Indeed I do,' Mrs Bunn swung a small backpack off her back and rummaged around in it, drawing out a pile of silvery, metallic material.

'Put one of these on each, girls,' Mrs Bunsen commanded, picking one up and tying it round her own waist. 'They've been specially treated to deflect any hot sparks and explosions.'

'I'm putting one over my face,' Cleo draped one over her head. 'There's no way I'm risking *these* looks for a stupid science experiment.'

'You never know, if a spark flies through your ear and into your brain it might make you MORE intelligent,' Arabella said. Cleo growled but the apron stayed firmly over her head.

Mrs Bunsen rolled her eyes.

'I have a pair of special glasses for each of you for that very reason, Cleo,' she said, swinging her backpack off and lifting a bunch of thick plastic spectacles out of it. She threw a pair at Cleo. 'Here, take that apron off your head and put these on, then at least you'll be able to see. These are specially designed goggles that will shield your eyes.' #Clever invention. #SO funny to look at.

Soon, we were all standing in a group, looking like a bunch of mad scientists, wearing aprons and giant plastic goggles. Mrs Bunsen bent over and rummaged around at the bottom of her backpack, drawing out three curious looking bottles and a shiny container. Mrs Bunn just stared out across the sea at the horizon. I thought she was probably bored, wishing she was back at school drinking a nice, hot cup of tea.

'Our secret ingredients,' Mrs Bunsen brandished the bottles and container above her head. 'Cardomina, Belzum and Raducci, and a mixing bowl made from Sparkozi. I think we'll have a quick practise now, maybe test out small amounts of the chemicals, then break for lunch. After all we need to make sure we have enough energy ourselves if we're going to be conducting nuclear experiments, don't we?'

'Nuclear what?' Mrs Bunn's eyes snapped away from the horizon and focused on Mrs Bunsen.

'Oh for goodness sake, you haven't changed a bit, have you Andromida? You were always on about nuclear experiments as a child. I remember when you blew up dad's greenhouse trying to split the atom. His prize cucumbers were in there, you know, it affected him very badly. He never entered another garden show again.'

'As a child? What, do you mean you're sisters?' Arabella asked, eyes widening.

'Haven't you told them we're related, Andromida?' Mrs Bunn's eyes stopped looking all twinkly and narrowed so that she looked rather spiteful.

'No, Hilda,' Mrs Bunsen said quietly. 'And this is neither the time nor the place to go into it. Right, first years, there's been a change of plan. We'll break for an early lunch now, and resume our experiment in forty five minutes time. Please take great care of your goggles and aprons, they're very expensive.'

Well gosh and golly and blow me down with a feather, I wasn't expecting *that* revelation! But now that I look at them they do look rather similar, although Mrs Bunn's eyes are darker and deeper than Mrs Bunsen's and she always looks rather untidy as though she's just been blown through a hedge backwards, whereas Mrs Bunsen's SUCH a neat dresser. Right, must go now, Diary, as Arabella and I are going off to find a nice spot on the beach to eat our packed lunches.

Later on the beach, Tuesday, 7th February

Curious happenings, Diary...

Wow, what a day. Arabella and I went and sat in the mouth of a really sweet little cave to eat our packed lunches, so we could look out to sea and be protected from the breeze at the same time. We'd talked about Mrs Bunsen and Mrs Bunn and how unexpected the whole thing was, and were half way through our smoked salmon and avocado sandwiches, when Arabella said,

'Look over there. What on *earth* is Mrs Bunn doing?' I looked where she was pointing and saw the dinner lady looking out to sea, doing what looked like some very strange exercises. First she stuck her right arm up in the air and her left one out horizontally, then she swapped them round. Before long she was twirling her arms as though she was pretending to be a windmill. #Talk about odd.

'I have no idea what she's doing,' I said, giggling. 'But she does look *very* funny. Maybe she's trying to keep fit or something. We watched for a bit longer, drinking our fizzy grape juice, nudging each other and giggling every now and again because Mrs

Bunn really *did* look like she was doing an exercise routine in time with the waves.

Arabella looked at her watch, then scrambled to her feet.

'Time to go,' she reached out and helped me up. 'Come on, I can't *wait* to do this experiment.'

'Yes,' I said, feeling very doubtful, wiping the sand off my glasses and apron then traipsing after her.

'Gather round,' Mrs Bunsen shouted as we joined the huddled group of first years on the other side of the beach. 'Make sure everyone's standing where they can see because I'm going to talk you through the experiment and do a demonstration, then ask you to split into groups so you can try the experiment for yourselves. Goggles on everybody? Then here we go.'

She unscrewed the caps of the three bottles. One gave a hiss, one oozed green smoke and the other frothed over. Cleo and Clarice took several paces back. Mrs Bunsen stepped forwards, placing the mixing bowl in the centre of our circle.

'One drop of Cardomina,' she said, shaking a thick bright blue glob from the bottle that had hissed. It landed in the middle of the mixing bowl with a "SSssssss". 'Three shakes of Belzum,' Mrs Bunsen's eyes lit up in a way I'd never seen before as she gently prized out three feathery drops of green goo, making sure they landed on top of the Cardomina. Nothing happened. 'And four healthy squeezes of Raducci,' she said, whacking a load of deep pink froth on top of the contents of the mixing bowl.

White light shot upwards from the depths of the bowl, causing most of us to fall over backwards in shock. Only Arabella was left standing, her mouth open, a look of adoration in her eyes. As the light arced it turned into a fountain of pink, green and blue sparkles that rained down on us. Clarice and Cleo screamed and ran into the tunnel and I must say I was glad to be wearing my safety goggles because the sparks were so bright they made my eyes hurt a bit, but they didn't seem to do my hair any harm, just made it smell smoky for hours afterwards.

'And there you have it,' Mrs Bunsen came forwards, rubbing her hands together when the sparks had died out, her eyes still alive. 'A simple yet effective experiment, dangerous if you haven't been listening. A source of energy made from splitting the atoms of a few simple ingredients. Remember, one drop of Cardomina, three shakes of Belzum and four healthy squeezes of Raducci. Now split into pairs, collect a mixing bowl from Mrs Bunn's backpack and spread out along the beach to conduct your own experiments.' #Woo hoo!

Arabella took charge of our science experiment and told me *exactly* what to do and how many drops to squeeze out of each bottle, which I was quite glad about because otherwise I might have blown up the whole beach, although it was a *bit* annoying how bossy she became at the end. We practised making the fountain of light and sparks loads of times in different parts of the beach. Arabella made one that went half way up the cliff! Fountains of all shapes and sizes were going off all around us the whole time; Lynne and Moira made quite a good one, Lottie and Erica's was quite small – Arabella says they probably didn't use *quite* enough Raducci – and Cleo and Clarice went wrong with theirs and managed to set the end of Clarice's hair on fire, which she screamed and screamed about. #Really loud voice. #Hurt my ears.

At the moment, I'm sitting on the beach drinking hot chocolate with the rest of the first years.

Mrs Bunn brewed some up for us as a treat on the portable stove she brought in her backpack, as she said we'd worked so hard all day. *And* she gave us all one of her chewy, strawberry sweets. She's rather sweet really, let us sit down to drink it while she went round collecting up all the goggles and aprons.

Right, I have to go now Diary, Mrs Bunsen is calling for us to troop off down the tunnel and back to school. Cleo and Clarice are first in line, I don't think they've enjoyed today very much!

Later that night, Tuesday 7th February

Crisis, Diary!

Oh my goodness, you'll never guess what happened while we were all at the beach, it's SUCH a disaster, especially for poor Arabella.

As we dragged ourselves up the last bit of the

tunnel and into the kitchen cellars, VERY tired after our day on the beach, we could hear frantic shouting that got louder and louder as we got closer to the kitchens.

'Is that...Marcel?' Melody asked from behind me.

'Yes,' I said, worried. 'I think it is.' We all know Marcel has a TERRIBLY bad temper and always argues with his chefs, but sometimes I think it's all for show. He has a really soft side too and always bakes amazing cakes for all the teachers, pupils and chefs on their birthdays. But the way he was shouting now was different from normal, he sounded more anguished and distressed.

'Where are all the jars of Italian sweets?' Arabella said as we walked through the deepest cellar. 'I'm sure they were right *here* before.' She pointed to a large, dark space on the floor.

'Maybe Marcel moved things around while we were out?' I said, doubt creeping into my stomach. Something didn't feel right at all.

'It certainly looks a lot more spacious down here than it did this morning,' Lottie said, coming to walk next to me. 'Don't you think?'

'Yes,' I said, breaking into a run, seeing the steps up to the kitchen ahead of me. I arrived in the shiny silver and white kitchen, closely followed by Arabella and Lottie, in time to hear Marcel shriek,

'But where 'as it all gone, Mrs Fairchild? Where are all my INGREDIENTS?'

'Deep breaths, Marcel, there's a lamb,' Mrs Fairchild said in a calm little voice. She was standing in front of the enormous oven, hands clasped, watching Marcel pace up and down the kitchen. For once he wasn't wearing his chef's hat, which was a bit alarming to see because Marcel ALWAYS wears his hat, it's practically part of him. But most disturbing of all were the tears that ran down his face in rivers.

'Why would anyone 'ere do theez to me?' He howled. 'Why, Mrs Fairchild. Why? What did I do to deserve it? All my new batch of ingredients stolen, including ze WHOLE stock of Italian sweets. The school meals are ruined. RUINED!'

'You are a great chef, Marcel,' Mrs Fairchild stepped forwards, taking his hand and holding it tight. She glanced up and saw us first years assembling at the top of the steps. I'm sure half our mouths must have been hanging open. 'I know you'll be able to manage with the ingredients you have left until we catch the culprit and get back what is rightfully yours and the schools.'

'The Italian sweets,' whispered Arabella in my ear. 'Please don't tell me they've been stolen.

They're the most important ingredient of Magic Mousse.'

I turned to see she'd gone rather pale. Like I mentioned before, Arabella SERIOUSLY loves Magic Mousse.

'Look,' Mrs Fairchild let go of Marcel's hand and shooed him gently towards the kitchen door. 'Why don't you go to bed, there's a dear? Things always look better after a good night's sleep. Let's talk about this again tomorrow morning.' So with his head hanging down, Marcel shuffled off into the corridor, sniffing loudly. Mrs Fairchild turned to us.

'I didn't mean for you to see or hear any of that,' she said, quite seriously for her. 'Please understand, first years, that something extremely serious happened while you were out on your school trip today, and I shall be calling an emergency assembly about it tomorrow morning. The fact is, most of Marcel's ingredients that he keeps in the cellars have gone missing, presumed stolen. The total amount they are worth together is over a hundred thousand pounds, as Marcel buys in the finest, rarest foods from around the world.'

Mrs Bunn, who'd come to stand behind me – I could tell from the chewing and strawberry sweet aroma - tutted loudly. Arabella moaned softly, her worst fears confirmed. Mrs Fairchild stopped frowning.

'But let's not forget its only food that we're talking about,' she rubbed her hands together. 'Luckily it's all replaceable. Eventually. Rather an expensive batch to buy back, but never mind. Now come on, off to bed with you all. You must be tired after your busy day.'

Well. Really! #What a palava!

Wednesday, 8th February

The plot thickens, Diary.

By breakfast time, the whole school seemed to know what had happened.

There was a buzz in the dining room as we ate our smoked mackerel on seeded toast with lemon mayonnaise. Literally EVERYONE seemed to be talking about it.

'Apparently Marcel's scream made Mrs Fairchild sprint from her office...'

'They're calling the police in, there's a criminal amongst us...'

'ALL of the Italian sweets are gone, Marcel will never be able to make Magic Mousse again...'

'Noooo!' Arabella yelled, when she heard this remark.

Marcel came out of the kitchen to talk to Mrs Fairchild, who was sitting on a table not far from our own. He didn't look like the chef we'd come to know and love, his face was pale, his eyes looked down and his shoulders sagged. *Poor* Marcel. I was annoyed to see Clarice and Cleo intercepting him on his way over. Whatever they said to him made him shake his head vigorously and look even more miserable. #So whingy.

'Meesus Fairchild,' he cried, as he got nearer to the headmistress's table. 'Those blonde 'aired girls just told me they think ze thief is Franco, as e's new and nothing like this ever 'appened before 'e arrived. But I've known Franco since 'e was born. I can't believe –'

Mrs Fairchild sighed.

'I believe you may be talking about Cleo and Clarice, Marcel, and if I'm not mistaken, Franco accidentally poured mint sauce all over Clarice's white top the other night.' Her eyes twitched mischievously. 'Let's not forget that this may be *why* those particular girls are so quick to point the finger at Franco, to exact some sort of petty revenge.'

Marcel shook his head despairingly.

'I 'aven't slept all night,' he said, wringing his hands. 'I just don't know what to theenk anymore. Maybe I should resign-'

'Don't you dare,' Mrs Fairchild said, rather fiercely for her. 'You and I shall be brave and stick together, Marcel. If we do that, and with the help of the police – who I'll ring later today - we'll somehow get to the bottom of this mystery once and for all. And today we'll buy back at least some of your ingredients and keep them under lock and key until the thief has been caught. Deal?' She stuck her hand out. Marcel sighed.

'Deal,' he said. 'Thank you, Meesus Fairchild. You are indeed a magnificent lady.' Mrs Fairchild twinkled and giggled in reply.

Arabella turned to me.

'We should investigate too,' she said in a low voice. 'This is the worst crisis I've ever faced. I think I might *die* if I can never eat Magic Mousse again.' I grinned. She can be so melodramatic sometimes.

'OK,' I said. 'What shall we do?'

'We need to take a look at the scene of the crime ourselves,' Arabella muttered. 'Take a look at the cellars without a grown up breathing down our necks. That way-'

'What are you two whispering about?' Mrs Bunn came waddling over, a beam on her face but her eyes sharp like usual. 'Come on, eat up or you'll be late for lessons.'

Right, I must go now Diary as I have a double art lesson after break. Arabella and I have agreed to do some snooping around in the cellars after school today. I just hope we don't get caught...

Later that afternoon, Wednesday 8th February

Disturbing discoveries, Diary!

My goodness, we've had an exciting day.

Basically, after lessons finished we wandered down to the kitchens looking really innocent. Our cover story was that we needed some chocolate as we were feeling tired after all our hard work, and were looking for a chef to ask him for some. But really, we were determined to sneak down to the cellars and have a look around to see if we could find a clue that might tell us who the thief is.

Luckily there was no one about, which is exactly what we'd hoped for. We knew the chefs tended to take a break between lunch and dinner time as we'd often seen them strolling about the school gardens arm in arm, or sometimes arguing loudly, so it was an eerily quiet kitchen we found ourselves sneaking into.

'Excellent,' Arabella whispered. 'Let's go.'

We tiptoed over to the cellar door and descended the stairs. Arabella had a torch stuffed up her cardigan sleeve, which THANK GOODNESS she got out and shone in front of us or I think I might have tripped.

As before, the cellars looked remarkably empty.

'They must be locking any new ingredients up somewhere safe,' I whispered.

'Yep,' Arabella whispered back, sounding grim. 'Marcel won't leave anything to chance now there's a thief about. Come on, let's go down to the deepest cellar where the Italian sweets were kept. You never know, we might find a clue...'

I gulped, but kept following her. Arabella is much braver than me and she doesn't mind the dark that much but I have to say I *did* find the cellars a *little* bit scary, especially as it was just me, Arabella and a torch and lots and lots of darkness. We didn't dare put the wall lamps on in case it attracted the attention of any visitors to the kitchen.

I was just beginning to think I might have to run back up to the kitchens when Arabella said,

'Wait! What was that?'

'Um?' I said.

'Listen,' she said, moving her feet around. 'Car

you hear that crunching sound?'

I listened carefully.

'Actually, I can,' I said. 'What is it?' I moved my own feet around and found I could make crunching noises too.

'That's odd,' Arabella said. I could tell she was bending down because the torch light bent down too. 'Ooh, it feels all grainy.' She stood up and shone the torch on her hand.

'Crushed up Italian sweets,' I breathed.

Arabella shone her torch down on the ground and I IMMEDIATELY saw a trail of crushed and stamped on sweets that led away from where we stood. I took her arm.

'Arabella, follow the trail of sweets, it may lead us to another clue.' I was feeling more excited than scared at this point. 'The thief might have recently moved their loot!'

'Good idea,' she muttered. Together, we crunched after the trail which led us right up to the OLD SMUGGLING TUNNEL'S DOOR!

We looked at each other. I could tell by the light of the torch that Arabella's eyes were rather wide and I saw her gulp a couple of times. Personally, my heart was going crazily fast and I felt rather dizzy.

'I think we should go down the tunnel,' Arabella said in a strangely high pitched voice.

'But it might be dangerous,' I said quickly, not relishing the thought of going down the murky, slimy tunnel again. 'If the thief's there we might find ourselves in serious trouble.'

'But if we don't,' Arabella's eyes turned pleading. 'We may miss a vital clue and lose all the Italian sweets and Marcel might resign and then I'll

NEVER HAVE MAGIC MOUSSE AGAIN!'

'Sshhh!' I said, squeezing her arm. The LAST
thing we needed was to be discovered snooping
around in the cellars. *'Calm down*. OK, we'll go down
the tunnel a bit but if there's any sign of danger I
think we should come straight back. OK?'

'OK,' Arabella said. 'Give me a leg up and I'll
get Marcel's key down.'

Within minutes we were walking, or should I
say CRUNCHING, down the tunnel again. Arabella had
insisted on closing the door to the cellar, saying it
would look less suspicious if one of the chefs had to
come down for some reason. To be honest, I hated
every minute of the journey through the tunnel that
time and it seemed even longer and murkier than last
time. I kept having to remind myself of how upset
Arabella and Marcel would be if the mystery was
never solved.

AT LAST we came to the mouth of the tunnel, finding ourselves once more on Little Pineham beach, the winter sun beginning to set behind the grey horizon.

'Look Arabella,' I said, immediately spotting a pile of large cardboard boxes stacked up against the side of the cliff. 'What on earth are those?'

Checking around us for signs of movement, we crept over to the boxes. The top one was open and we both peeked in.

'Jars of Italian sweets!' Arabella half shouted.

'Sshhh!' I said, feeling quite cross. 'I'm not exactly enjoying being here, Arabella, and the least you could do is keep your voice down so we don't get discovered if the thief is somewhere about.'

'Sorry,' she whispered, looking sheepish. 'I was just so excited to see them.'

I rolled my eyes and grinned. We lifted up the jars of Italian sweets, finding that several had smashed and were half empty – explaining the trail of sweets we'd followed. We also found other ingredients that had been thieved, including jars of rare herbs and Moroccan pasta swirls. As we packed the ingredients back together, trying to make it look like they hadn't been touched, a small piece of paper floated off the top of the box and fluttered down to the sand. Arabella picked it up.

'Oh,' she said.

'What is it?' I asked, busy packing jars on top of herbs.

'It looks like one of Mrs Bunn's strawberry sweet wrappers,' Arabella said slowly. 'Look.' I looked over and yes indeed, it was one of the dinner lady's trade mark bright pink sweet wrappers.

'She might have dropped one by mistake when

we were doing the science experiment,' I said, feeling uncertain. 'And...the wind might have blown it on top of the box. Anyway, it can't have been Mrs Bunn who raided the cellar that day, she was on the beach with us the whole time.'

'You're right,' Arabella said, looking relieved. After all Mrs Bunn *had* been very nice to us, sharing her sweets and everything. It wasn't pleasant thinking of her being a criminal.

We tramped back to the mouth of the tunnel, keeping watch all the time. Just as we got there, my foot slipped. I looked down.

'Mud!' I whispered. 'What on earth is mud doing on a beach, Arabella?'

She looked down.

'I can't believe we didn't notice this when we arrived,' she said in a low voice, looking puzzled. 'Thi mystery is getting stranger and stranger. At least we have several proper clues now; the trail of sugar down the tunnel, the boxes of ingredients on the beach and the strange patches of mud near the start of the tunnel. Do you think-'

'What on earth is THAT?' I cut across her, suddenly seeing a gleaming, unusual object lying in the tide mark on the sand, quite near to where we stood. In a minute I'd nipped over and picked it up, bringing it back for us both to examine.

'It's a beautiful bottle,' Arabella said, stroking its glassy, violet sides.

'I think there's something in it,' I said, pulling out the cork and shaking it upside down. A tight roll of paper plopped out.

Arabella picked it up and unrolled it.

'"We'll meet at midnight sharp. We sail at

quarter past",' she read.

'I think we need to go and see Mrs Fairchild right now,' I said, looking around, suddenly feeling VERY uncomfortable. 'I don't like this, Arabella. If that note is meant for the thief, they might still be around expecting to find the note or worse still, we might meet them in the tunnel!'

'Ooh, I hadn't thought of that,' Arabella went a shade paler. 'Right, let's go.' She stuffed the note back in the bottle and dropped it and we set off down the tunnel at a canter, not speaking until half an hour later when we popped back into the school's deepest cellar, EXTREMELY tired and out of breath.

Even though we were hungry and thirsty, we decided to go STRAIGHT to Mrs Fairchild's study and tell her EVERYTHING we'd found out.

When we'd knocked and heard her high little voice trill, 'Come in,' we found her lying in a hammock, suspended from two hooks on her ceiling. She was swinging from side to side.

'Oh hello my dears,' she said warmly, hopping elegantly off the side. 'Just testing my jungle equipment. I'm going on safari during the next school holidays, and I've always thought it's very important to break your hammock in first, don't you think?'

'Er, yes?' I hazarded. 'Listen, Mrs Fairchild, Arabella and I have been doing a spot of investigating into the food theft and we think we may have found some clues.'

'Ah, my resident detectives,' Mrs Fairchild gave us a beaming smile and signalled that we should sit down on her sofa. 'I was hoping you might accept the case.' I smiled, pleased she trusted us after our previous adventures at Egmont. 'Do make yourselves comfortable and tell me all about it, my dears.'

So we did. We told her all about sneaking

down to the cellars, (she raised her eyebrows but didn't say anything) and how we'd found a trail of glittery Italian sweet style sugar there that led to the door of the tunnel. We explained how we'd gone down the tunnel to the beach, (her eyebrows went even higher) and found the boxes of food, patches of mud and a note in an exotic, unusual looking bottle.

'It said something like, "We'll meet at midnight sharp. We'll sail at quarter past",' I said.

'Yes,' Arabella agreed. 'Oh and we found one of Mrs Bunn's sweet wrappers on top of the boxes of ingredients but we thought the wind had probably blown it there after she dropped it during the science trip.'

'Hmmm,' Mrs Fairchild leaned forwards, her eyes narrowing. 'It seems like there's only one possible course of action. We need to organise a stake out for tonight.'

'What do you mean?' I asked.

'It sounds like that note was meant for the thief who has smuggled our goods to the beach, my dears,' Mrs Fairchild said. 'I vote that you both join me, Marcel and of course some fine policemen from Little Pineham's police force - who I'll call directly - on the beach at Little Pineham tonight. We'll drive round there instead of walking through the tunnel in case we bump into the crooks, then hide ourselves somewhere on the beach to observe any funny going's on. Hopefully we'll catch the thief red handed.'

'Wow,' Arabella breathed. 'That sounds SO exciting, Mrs Fairchild.'

'Exciting, but also perhaps a little risky, my dear,' Mrs Fairchild said, her eyes beginning to twinkle again. 'But I do believe both of you are entitled to be there after all the detective work you've done.'

'Thank you,' I said, feeling rather thrilled.

On the way back to our dorm we bumped into the twins, Moira and Lynne. There were wearing wellies and carrying trowels.

'Hello, what have you been up to?' I asked, grinning at their unruly curls and freckly faces.

'Oh we've been helping Bertie the gardener and his new assistant with the weeding,' Lynne grinned. 'Need to go and have baths now though, don't we Moira? It's *so* muddy out there at the moment. See you at dinner time, girls.'

I have to go now, Diary. We have SO much to plan before our stake out tonight and apart from anything else, I'm STARVING! #Adventures make you hungry.

Thursday, 9th February

Smugglers, Diary – it's official!

What a night and with SUCH an unexpected ending!

Last night, Mrs Fairchild came over to whisper in our ears at dinner time.

'I'll come and knock for you at half past ten tonight,' she said. 'Wear sensible clothes, it's going to be very cold on the beach.' We both nodded.

Arabella and I tried to get some rest after dinner but to be honest we were both FAR too excited, so we watched television on our giant flat screen TV instead.

Luckily there was a good film showing, although I couldn't *really* concentrate on it, but it didn't seem too long before there was a soft knock at the door. Mrs Fairchild let herself in. She was wearing black army trousers, a black jumper, a thick black jacket and a black, woolly hat.

'It's time, girls,' she said, rubbing her wrinkly old hands together in excitement. 'Let's go and spot some smugglers.'

We pulled on our thick jackets, hats and wellies and tiptoed after her through the now quiet school. I could hear some girls already snoring their heads off as we passed their dorms.

The headmistress led us to her huge, sleek black car, which was parked at the front of the staff car park. Marcel was already sitting in the back seat, blowing on his fingers to warm them up.

"Ello my leetle detectives,' he said, ruffling our hair as we got in.

Mrs Fairchild drove smoothly out of the schoo gates and through the black countryside towards

Little Pineham. Within five minutes, we'd parked in a secluded spot hidden from the beach by a row of trees, and were walking across the moonlit sand. I saw the stack of smuggled ingredients still there, leaning against the side of the cliff.

'We're heading for that cave,' Mrs Fairchild whispered, pointing to the largest rocky hollow on the beach. 'Five police officers should already be there, I phoned them and arranged everything earlier today, after you left my study.'

Sure enough as we entered the cave, there was a polite cough.

'Evenin' Mrs Faichild,' a deep voice boomed softly from the back.

'Oh are you all here? How marvellous!' Mrs Fairchild trilled, as though she'd just arrived at a party. A torch flickered on in the deepest part of the cave and we peered through the flickering light to see five policemen all crouching down low, surrounded by an assortment of handcuffs and rope. It made me shiver with a mixture of fear and excitement to see them there.

We silently took up our positions, Arabella and I to one side of the cave, Mrs Fairchild and Marcel to the other.

'And now we just sit and wait,' the same policeman rumbled. 'And if there's any trouble I want you two youngsters to run to the back of this cave and wait till it's over. Is that clear?'

'Yes,' Arabella and I whispered together.

We stayed in our positions for what seemed like HOURS. At first I enjoyed watching the silvery, moonlit waves crashing over the shore, while keeping one eye out for any sign of movement on the beach. After a while my legs started to go numb and my fingers went so cold that I thought they might drop off.

After what seemed like AGES, things suddenly started to get interesting. A large-ish boat floated silently in to view, coming as close as it could to the shore. My heart went wild and there were stiffening noises around me as we all sat up and gave it our full attention.

Then, two figures came bumbling out of the mouth of the smuggling tunnel. One wore a bun in her hair and was grumbling loudly.

'Mrs Bunn,' I breathed. 'I can smell her strawberry sweets from here. But who is the other person?'

'Nick, the gardener's new helper,' Mrs Fairchild whispered, sounding unimpressed. 'I also happen to know that he's Mrs Bunn's nephew. She begged me to take him on when I gave her the job as dinner lady. Said he was a good worker and desperately needed to make some money to support him and his young wife. But now, it seems, they had darker plans in mind all along.'

The policemen shuffled forwards, coming parallel to us, ready to pounce at the right moment.

'Come on Nick, you useless lump,' we heard Mrs Bunn say crossly, as she directed her nephew towards the stack of ingredients. Her kind, mother hen type smile was now completely gone. 'Start heaving those boxes down to the sea. Your uncle's come to pick them up and we don't want to keep him waiting, do we? You know how cross he gets sometimes.'

'Can't you help?' Nick moaned, trying to shut the top of the first box then lifting it up and staggering off.

'Don't be cheeky, young man, you know how my back hurts if I pick up anything heavy,' Mrs Bunn popped another sweet into her mouth and chewed vigorously.

It was a painful sight, watching Nick struggle with box after box while Mrs Bunn ploughed through loads of sweets, while constantly telling him what he was doing wrong.

'Come on muscle man, lift the box higher, are you a man or a wimp? Not like *that*, Nick, all the food will fall out. Come on, be sensible!'

Eventually all the boxes were down at the water's edge with Mrs Bunn and Nick standing behind them, looking out to sea. Mrs Bunn started doing the strange arm movements and exercises that she'd done on the day of the science trip. Arabella and I giggled.

'Semaphore,' Mrs Fairchild whispered, sounding thoughtful. 'Very clever. She's using those signals as a way of communicating something to whoever is in that boat.'

We watched as a small rowing boat plopped over the side of the big boat and onto the rolling sea. A burly man with a thick, bushy beard climbed down after it and was soon rowing to shore.

'Come on, hurry up,' he said as he picked up a box and placed it in the boat. 'We've got to get out of here quick smart in case anyone spots us.'

'Posh idiots,' Mrs Bunn spat as she supervised more box lugging. 'Serves them right, they can easily buy themselves more luxury food, they have more money than sense, that lot.'

'Now,' said the policeman with the deep voice. The five policemen burst out of the cave and belted across the beach towards the little group of smugglers. Nick and the man from the boat surrendered at once but Mrs Bunn put up a fight, kicking at anyone who went near her and even throwing her current packet of sweets at a policeman's head.

It took three policemen to finally hold her down and arrest her but at last she was in handcuffs, held firmly either side by the two burliest policemen. #Blimey. #Strong woman.

'Come on Marcel,' Mrs Fairchild said, standing up and stretching. 'Let's go and get some answers before they take those crooks away.'

'Can we come?' I asked.

'Of course,' Mrs Fairchild said. 'We wouldn't have caught those rotters if it wasn't for you two.'

We followed our tiny headmistress and Marcel as they strode across the beach. Luckily the moon gave us enough light to see by as for once it wasn't hidden behind a cloud.

'Hello Hilda,' Mrs Fairchild's crisp words

punched through the night air as she took up position in front of Mrs Bunn. 'Perhaps you'd like to explain to Marcel why you and your nephew stole his batch of ingredients?'

Marcel pulled himself up straight, choosing to remain in dignified silence.

Mrs Bunn scowled unattractively.

'I should have known,' she spat, looking at me and Arabella. 'It's you two. Always muttering and whispering together like a pair of idiots.'

'That will do, Mrs Bunn,' Mrs Fairchild said calmly. 'Just explain your actions to us, if you'd be so kind.'

'I knew we were on to a good thing as soon as that sister of mine told me about her posh school,' Mrs Bunn growled.

'Your sister?' Mrs Fairchild repeated.

'Mrs Bunsen,' I said. 'We found out she was Mrs Bunn's sister during the science trip.'

'Shut it, clever cloggs,' Mrs Bunn glared at me. 'Anyway, as I was saying. Andromdia's always banging on about how *marvellous* Egmont is and how simply *wonderful* the meals are.' Marcel permitted himself a small smile. 'When she told me what some of the ingredients were, especially when she said Marcel made Magic Mousse once a week, I could feel a plan forming in my head. You see, Mr Bunn, my husband, once worked as the gardener's helper at Egmont many years ago and when I expressed an interest in the place he told me all about the secret passage he discovered that leads all the way from the school's kitchens to the beach.'

'Too right,' Mr Bunn said. 'That 'orrible man Bertie fired me twenty years ago. Said I was stealing logs to put on my fire.'

'And were you?' Mrs Fairchild enquired.

'Well yeah, but that's not the point. He shouldn't have accused me, it made me angry. I haven't had a proper job since.'

Mrs Fairchild rolled her eyes.

'So I did my sums and worked out that if we stole just one delivery of ingredients to your posh school, we could sell them for thousands and be set up for life.' Mrs Bunn's eyes gleamed as she recalled her cunning plan. 'And it would have worked out just fine too, if you lot hadn't stuck your big noses in,' she snapped, looking round.

'Take them away, officers,' Mrs Fairchild waved her hand dismissively, turning to walk away. 'Poor Mrs Bunsen, having a sister like that. No wonder she's never mentioned her before.'

'I'll get my ingredients back,' Marcel said

happily, watching an officer unload the box from the boat. 'I'm so happy I could cry.'

'Well please don't,' Mrs Fairchild tinkled cheerfully. 'You have to help me get these brave girls back to bed. Come on Marcel, you can tell Franco that his name has been cleared tomorrow morning.'

'Ah, leetle Franco,' Marcel said, springing across the beach, back to his usual self. 'I always knew he 'ad nothing to do with it.' He turned to me and Arabella. 'Girls, 'ow can I ever repay you for 'elping to find my food?'

'Er, actually, Marcel, I do have *one* idea,' Arabella said...

Friday, 10th February

I'm completely stuffed, Diary!

What a meal! Basically, last night, Arabella asked Marcel if he could make the BIGGEST pile of Magic Mousse in the world in order to celebrate the smugglers being caught. And he did! It was a work of art – a mound of mousse six feet high, literally dripping with glittery Italian sweets (which the police had returned during the night) and chocolatey, honeycomb yumminess. There was enough for each pupil and teacher in the whole school to have second and even third helpings. I don't think I'll EVER need to eat again!

Mrs Bunsen actually came up to me and Arabella and SMILED! We'd been worried that she might be cross with us for helping to catch her smuggler sister but in actual fact she kept *thanking* us for catching the old crook! Mrs Bunsen said her sister had always been insanely jealous of her for being able to pass exams easily and get good jobs away from the boring dump of a town they'd been brought up in. She'd become really sick of Mrs Bunn's behaviour and was glad her sister was now locked up safely, somewhere she might actually get proper help with all her jealousy problems. Fancy that!

When we got back to our dorm this evening feeling really full but very happy, there was a notice pinned to our door. It said,

Dearest Davina and Arabella,

I'm writing to you with news of recent teaching changes. Mr Fossil, your geography teacher, will be travelling back to Ni Island next week in order to conduct some research for a book he's writing about endangered animals. So we are lucky enough to have the famous explorer, Dr Adam Aardvark, coming to teach Geography at Egmont Exclusive Boarding School for a month! Excitingly, he'll be bringing his collection of wild animals and birds with him for you

all to study. Apparently his boa constrictor snake is

ever so friendly!

Congratulations on being brave detectives once

again,

Much love as always,

Mrs Fairchild

'

Made in the USA
Lexington, KY
10 June 2017